APRIL FOOL, PHYLLIS!

by

Susanna Leonard Hill

illustrated by

Jeffrey Ebbeler

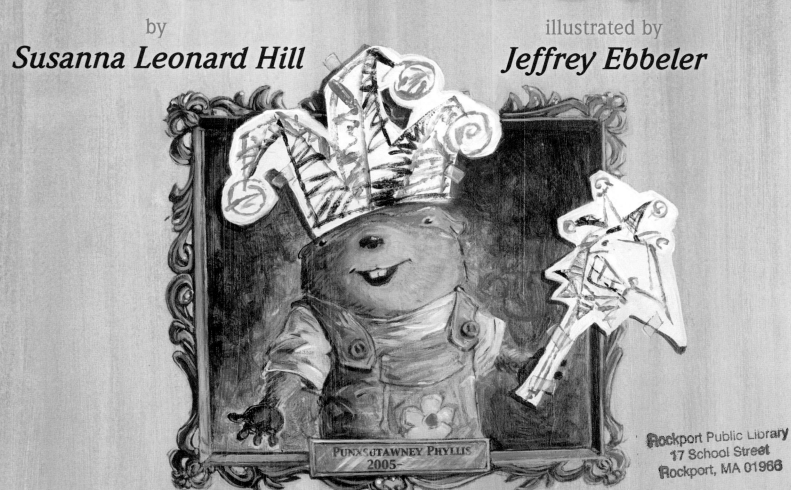

PUNXSUTAWNEY PHYLLIS
2005

HOLIDAY HOUSE / NEW YORK

HOLIDAY HOUSE is registered in the U.S. Patent and Trademark Office.
Printed and Bound in November 2010 at Tien Wah Press,
Johor Bahru, Johor, Malaysia.
The text typeface is Weidemann Medium.
The artwork for this book was made with acrylic paint.
www.holidayhouse.com
First Edition
1 3 5 7 9 10 8 6 4 2

Library of Congress Cataloging-in-Publication Data
Hill, Susanna Leonard.
April Fool, Phyllis! / by Susanna Leonard Hill ;
illustrated by Jeffrey Ebbeler. — 1st ed.
p. cm.
Summary: When Punxsutawney Phyllis forecasts a blizzard on April Fools' Day
the same day as the Spring Treasure Hunt—the other groundhogs are convinced
that Phyllis is pulling a prank. Includes information of the origins of April Fools'
Day and how it is celebrated around the world.
ISBN 978-0-8234-2270-8 (hardcover)
[1. Woodchuck—Fiction. 2. April Fools' Day—Fiction. 3. Weather forecasting—
Fiction. 4. Treasure hunt (Game)—Fiction.] I. Ebbeler, Jeffrey, ill. II. Title.
PZ7.H55743Ap2011
[E]—dc22
2010019878

PUNXSUTAWNEY PHIL
1939-1952

PUNXSUTAWNEY PHIL
1953-1974

PUNXSUTAWNEY PHIL
1778-1812

PUNXSUTAWNEY PHIL
1990-2004

PUNXSUTAWNEY PHIL
1823-1842

PUNXSUTAWNEY PHIL
1980-1989

PUNXSUTAWNEY PHIL
1900-1901

With love
for Becca, Ethan, and Garrick,
Sister and brothers extraordinaire

And for Penelope, whose day this is
S. L. H.

For Jack and Molly
J. E.

Phyllis knew everything about the weather.

After all, she was Punxsutawney Phyllis, Weather Prophet Extraordinaire!

So when she woke up on April first, the day of the Spring Treasure Hunt, it took only one whiff of the morning air to tell her something wasn't right.

"We have to cancel the treasure hunt," she announced at breakfast. "There's a blizzard coming!"

Everyone was stunned!

"A blizzard?" said Uncle Phil. "In April?"

Then Phil Junior started to laugh. "You actually had me fooled for a second," he said.

"Yeah, Phyllis," snickered Pete. "Not a bad joke!"

"This isn't an April Fools' joke," insisted Phyllis, but no one paid any attention.

Aunt Patsy flooded her pancakes with homemade maple syrup and passed the jug to old Grandfather Groundhog.

"What a great year for syrup!" he said. "I can't remember a year when the sap has run this long."

"That's because winter isn't over," said Phyllis. "I'm telling you, we're going to have a blizzard. Today!"

"Give up, Phyllis," said Pete.

"If folks don't listen," Phyllis said, "they'll be in danger when the blizzard comes."

A bit later, Phil Junior came in from outside.

"Phyllis is right!" he said. "It's freezing!" He held out his paws to Aunt Patsy.

"They're like icicles!" she exclaimed. "We can't have the treasure hunt if it's this cold!"

"I told you . . . ," began Phyllis.

"April Fool!" shouted Phil Junior. "I used a bag of ice to make my paws cold!"

"Very funny," said Phyllis. But everyone else laughed.

A few minutes later Pete yelled down from the mouth of the burrow, "Phyllis really was right! It's snowing!"

Everyone rushed up the tunnel. Sure enough, a curtain of fat white flakes drifted across the opening.

"Oh, my!" exclaimed Aunt Sassy.

"April Fool!" shouted Pete. "It's only confetti!"

"Make all the jokes you like," said Phyllis. "Just cancel the treasure hunt so no one gets lost in the snow."

But nobody listened.

The grown-ups sat in the sun outside the burrow to swap
tall tales and sent the youngsters off on the treasure hunt.
"Hmm," said Phyllis, reading the first clue.

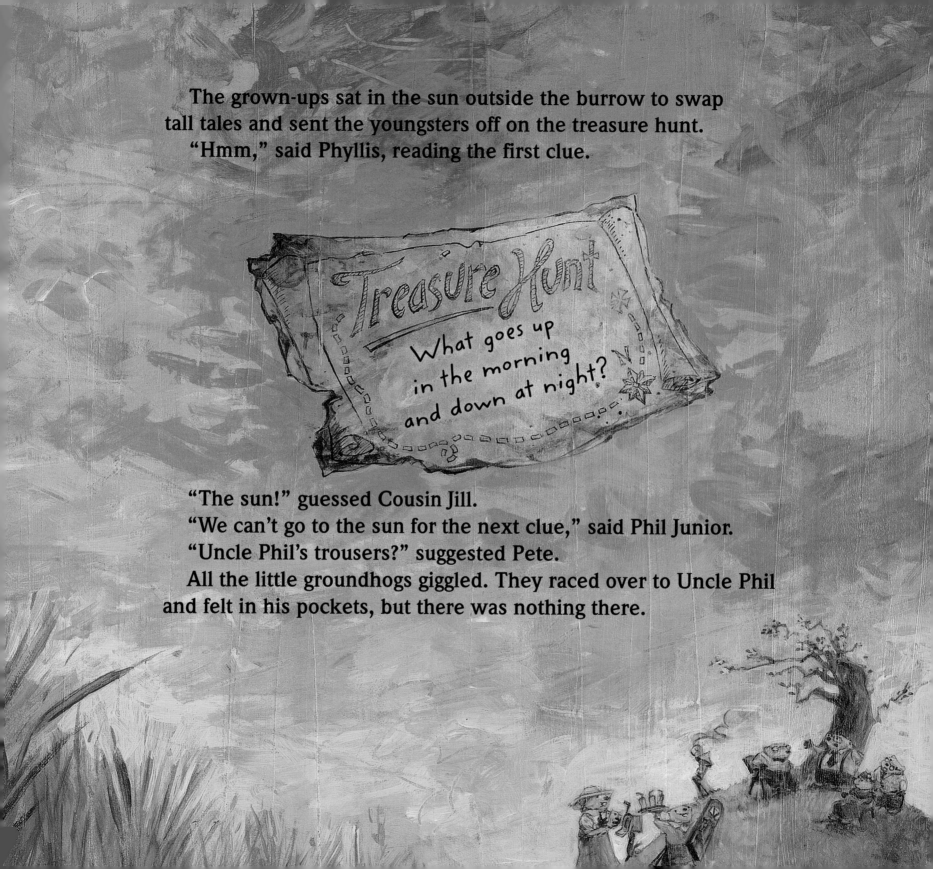

Treasure Hunt

What goes up
in the morning
and down at night?

"The sun!" guessed Cousin Jill.
"We can't go to the sun for the next clue," said Phil Junior.
"Uncle Phil's trousers?" suggested Pete.
All the little groundhogs giggled. They raced over to Uncle Phil
and felt in his pockets, but there was nothing there.

"There must be something else," said Jill.
"How about the thermometer?" suggested
Phyllis.
They hurried to the thermometer by the
door of the sugarhouse.

Inside, the big kettle still filled the air with sweet maple steam even though it was April.

"Oooh, it's nice and warm in here," said Cousin Willis. No one noticed that the thermometer had dropped below thirty degrees. All they saw was the second clue!

"What does this one say?" demanded Phil Junior.

Phyllis read:

What runs but has no legs?

"A clock!" said Pete.
     But the third clue was nowhere near the grandfather clock.

"An engine?" said Phil Junior.
     But no one knew of any engines in Punxsutawney Hollow.

"I know!" shouted Willis. "The stream!"
They all rushed down to the stream.

There was clue number three!

The young groundhogs followed the clues farther and farther—to the tree house, to the blackberry patch, and to the shore of Punxsutawney Pond.

"This must be the last one," Phyllis said. She brushed snowflakes out of her eyes to read the clue.

Treasure Hunt

What's sticky and sweet
and found in a tree?

"That's easy!" said Jill.

They all dashed for the honey tree.

"There it is!" shouted Willis, jumping up and down.

"What do you think it'll be?" Phil Junior asked as he lifted the lid.

It was another note!

Treasure Hunt

April Fool! You win but lose.
Look again at all your clues.
They can all be solved, you see,
With one answer, and it's me!

"I don't get it," said Pete.

Phyllis explained. "It means that there's one thing that's the answer to *all* the clues. But right now we have a bigger problem. Look at the snow!"

It was a problem indeed, falling thick and fast, making it impossible to see more than a few feet in any direction.

"How will we find our way home?" worried Willis.

Phyllis looked at the little groundhogs. They were depending on her to get them home safely. How was she going to do it?

All Phyllis could see was swirling white, and something flapping in the wind against a nearby sugar maple. The sap line!

"That's it!" she cried. "Everybody stay with me!"

The groundhogs clung to the sap line. Phyllis led the way from maple tree to maple tree, all the way back to the sugarhouse.

"Thank goodness you're back!" cried Aunt Patsy.

"We should have known you were right about the blizzard," said Uncle Phil. "Looks like we're the April Fools!"

"All's well that ends well," said Aunt Sassy.

"But we never solved the treasure hunt," said Phil Junior.

"Yes, we did!" Phyllis said triumphantly. "What goes up in the morning and down at night, what runs but has no legs, and what's sticky and sweet and found in a tree? SAP! The treasure is right here!"

Sure enough, in the back corner of the sugarhouse was another treasure chest.

Phyllis lifted the lid eagerly.

"It's empty!" she cried.

WHAT?

All the groundhogs crowded in to look.

"APRIL FOOL!" shouted Phyllis, and she tossed handfuls of maple candy in the air for everyone to share!

APRIL FOOLS' DAY

No one knows exactly when the first April Fools' Day took place, but it seems to have grown out of celebrations for the beginning of spring.

Long ago, the vernal equinox (first day of spring) was thought to occur on March 25 (instead of March 20 or 21). Some European cultures celebrated the coming of spring for eight days, beginning on March 25 and ending on April 1. This was New Year's Day according to the old Julian calendar. In 1582 Pope Gregory XIII established the Gregorian calendar, which we still use today, and New Year's Day was moved to January 1. Because news traveled slowly in those days, many people did not hear of the change immediately and continued to celebrate New Year's Day on April 1. Others heard of the change but didn't like it and stubbornly continued to celebrate New Year's Day on April 1. These people were thought of as fools. They were sent on "fools' errands," and people played practical jokes on them. Over time playing pranks on April 1 became a tradition.

In Scotland, April 1 has been celebrated by "hunting the gowk" (a gowk is a cuckoo or fool). Scotland is the origin of the "kick me" sign taped to people's backs.

In France, a favorite trick was to place a dead fish on someone's back without being noticed! When the prank was discovered, the prankster would yell, "*Poisson d'avril!*" Nowadays, French children substitute a paper cutout of a fish for the real thing. The person fooled is called a "*poisson d'avril*" (literally, April's fish). A fish may have been chosen for the joke because in April the sun leaves Pisces, the sign of the fish; but it was more likely because an April fish is young and hence easily caught.

The Jewish celebration of Purim is a similar spring prank-playing day.

In Iran, people play jokes on April 3 because it is the thirteenth day of the Persian calendar's new year, and it is believed that by going out you escape the bad luck of number 13.

In some countries, including Australia, Canada, New Zealand, and the United Kingdom, it is said that the prank must be played before midday. If it is played after midday, then the person pulling the prank is the fool!

April Fools' Day is a "just for fun" holiday. It is not religious, no one is expected to give candy or gifts, and no one is let off from work or school. It is simply a day for tricks and pranks. It is no wonder that such a day should occur when the promise of spring makes everyone lighthearted. But watch out or you could be the April Fool!

4/11